P MIT
Mitton, David, ill.
Meet Thomas the tank engine and his friends

DATE DUE	BORROWER'S NAME
	MICHAEL
DEC 05 '03	FRANK
SEP 2 7	
OCT 21 '04	

P MIT
Mitton, David, ill.
Meet Thomas the tank engine and his friends

Meet
Thomas the Tank Engine
and His Friends

Based on *The Railway Series* by the Rev. W. Awdry

**Photographs by David Mitton, Kenny McArthur, and
Terry Permane for Britt Allcroft's production of
*Thomas the Tank Engine and Friends***

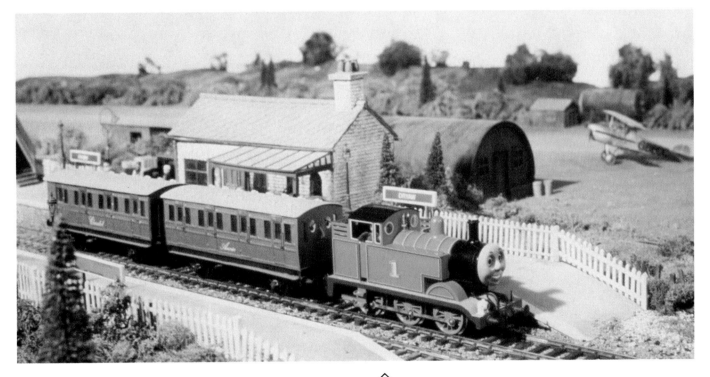

Random House 🏠 New York

Copyright © 1989 by William Heinemann Ltd. Photographs copyright © 1985, 1986 by Britt Allcroft (Thomas) Ltd. All rights reserved under International and Pan-American Copyright Conventions. Published in the United States by Random House, Inc., New York. All publishing rights: William Heinemann Ltd., London. All television and merchandising rights licensed by William Heinemann Ltd. to Britt Allcroft (Thomas) Ltd. exclusively, worldwide.

Library of Congress Cataloging-in-Publication Data:
Meet Thomas the tank engine and his friends / photographs by Kenny McArthur, David Mitton, and Terry Permane. p. cm. "Based on The railway series by the Rev. W. Awdry." SUMMARY: Sir Topham Hatt, in charge of all the railway engines on the Island of Sodor, introduces the various engines and the freight cars they pull, describing the personality of each. ISBN: 0-679-80102-2 (trade); 0-679-90102-7 (lib. bdg.) [1. Railroads— Trains—Fiction] I. McArthur, Kenny, ill. II. Mitton, David, ill. III. Permane, Terry, ill. IV. Awdry, W. Railway series. V. Thomas the tank engine and friends.
PZ7.M5133 1989 [E]—dc20 89-32299
Manufactured in the United States of America 6 7 8 9 10

Hello! Let me introduce myself. My name is Sir Topham Hatt. I'm in charge of all the railway engines here on the Island of Sodor.

When the engines aren't busy working, some of them rest in this shed at the Big Station.

Would you like to meet them? Well then, come along!

Meet Thomas the Tank Engine! He has six small wheels, a
short stumpy funnel, a short stumpy boiler, and a short
stumpy dome.

Thomas is a fussy little engine. All my engines are
important—but Thomas thinks none of them works as hard
as he does!

He used to collect coaches for the big engines to take on long journeys. After trains came in and all the passengers got off, he would push the coaches away so the engines could go and rest.

Now Thomas has two coaches of his own—*and* he is very proud to have his very own Branch Line!

Next I should like to introduce you to Annie and Clarabel. Annie only carries passengers. Clarabel can carry passengers, luggage, and a conductor.

One day Thomas was in such a hurry to leave the station, he forgot to wait for Clarabel's conductor to board. The conductor had to run to catch up with Thomas and the coaches!

Annie and Clarabel are rather old and need new paint. But Thomas doesn't mind that at all. The three of them like to sing songs to one another as they rattle along the line.

Do you know why Thomas was given his own Branch Line? Well, it was of course as a reward for helping another engine, named James.

Now meet James, an engine whose main job is to pull freight cars—but on his first day the silly freight cars pushed poor James down a hill into a field! It was Thomas who pulled away the freight cars and helped James back to the Engine Shed.

I was so pleased with Thomas. Now he was a Really Useful Engine! After the accident James got new brakes and a shiny coat of red paint. He now says that he is a Really Splendid Engine—one morning he let off steam so suddenly that he made my nice new top hat very wet.

Here's another engine who thinks he's special: Gordon, the
fastest and strongest of all my engines. He's proud of being
the only one strong enough to pull the express train.

But sometimes Gordon has to pull dirty freight cars filled
with coal, which makes him cross.

Once Gordon got stuck going up a hill, and he had to be
pushed from behind. We call it "Gordon's Hill" now!

Do you know who helped Gordon when he couldn't get up the hill? Edward—here he is—the kindest engine there is! I depend on Edward all the time. He calms everyone down.

When Edward pushed Gordon up the hill, everyone was very happy. Edward's driver gave him a drink of water and a new coat of blue paint with red stripes.

Edward even offered to help James with some mischievous freight cars one day—but James managed to keep them in line all by himself.

I asked Edward to train a new
engine to work in the yard. The
engine's name is Percy. Percy is a
tank engine. Thomas was so busy
working on his Branch Line and
Edward was so busy with the freight
cars that we needed a new tank
engine to get coaches ready for the
big engines to pull. I found Percy in
an Engine Workshop and chose
him myself.

Percy is little, but he can blow off steam very loudly. Sometimes he blows off steam just to surprise the bigger engines and make them jump! He enjoys playing jokes on them.

Here's an engine who thought he didn't need Edward's help—or anybody else's, either! Meet Henry, who went into a tunnel one rainy day and refused to come out. He said that the rain would ruin his green paint and red stripes!

Henry finally came out of the tunnel when Gordon burst a safety valve and couldn't pull his heavy coaches. It took Henry *and* Edward to pull Gordon's express train that day.

Henry now knows that the best way to keep his paint nice is to ask his driver to wipe him down at the end of the day!

You've heard about the freight cars—but have you met them yet? How silly and noisy they are! They talk a lot and don't pay attention to what they are doing. And freight cars love to play tricks on the engines.

One morning they pushed Thomas the Tank Engine down a hill, laughing and rattling the whole time. I told Thomas afterward that he had a lot to learn about freight cars.

Percy and Edward are quite good at making the freight cars behave. They love to push them into their proper places, even though the cars scream "Stop!"

Now here is Toby the Tram Engine. I met Toby when I was on vacation. With his cowcatcher in front and plates on the sides, Toby doesn't look like a steam engine at all!

Henrietta is Toby's coach, and she follows him everywhere. She and Toby used to take freight cars from farms and factories to the Main Line.

They ran on a special track alongside roads and through fields and towns. But as time went on, Toby had fewer freight cars and Henrietta had fewer passengers. So the track was closed down, and Toby and Henrietta came to work for me.

Now Toby and Henrietta go to the quarry every morning. James made fun of them at first because Toby and Henrietta looked old and shabby—but soon they were given new coats of paint. Now they look as good as new.

Well, now you've met Thomas and many of his friends. I think they are Really Useful Engines, don't you? Of course, not everyone here is a steam engine. Meet Bertie the Bus!

Bertie takes people who want to travel by train to Thomas— and Thomas brings people back to the station for Bertie to take home.

Once Bertie and Thomas had a race, and Thomas won. Bertie would have had to grow wings and fly if he wanted to beat Thomas over the hills!

Here is Harold the Helicopter, who *can* fly! He hovers like a
bird, by whirling his arms about.

Harold used to think that railways were slow and out-of-
date—in fact, not much use at all.

Then he and Percy had a race—
and guess who won? Percy—because
Harold couldn't find a place to land!
Now Harold is good friends with
all my engines, and they're always
happy to see him.

Here's another friend of Thomas's. Meet Terence the Tractor! Instead of train wheels Terence moves around on special wheels called caterpillars. They make it easy for him to go just about anywhere.

In the fall Terence plows fields. One winter day he rescued Thomas when the little engine got stuck in a pile of snow.

Terence the Tractor is slow and steady—and always has a smile ready!

I almost forgot to introduce you to some special people here: the engineers and conductors who operate the trains...and the signalmen who show the engines which way to go...and, of course, the passengers who ride in the coaches!

Now it's time to say good-bye. Thomas and his friends whistle "Peep, peep! Good-bye!" back to you.

Come and visit us again soon on the Island of Sodor!